DRAGLINS

For Sam, who likes collecting things,
with love x
VF

For Shelley, with love
CF

ORCHARD BOOKS
338 Euston Road, London NW1 3BH
Orchard Books Australia
Level 17/207, Kent Street, Sydney, NSW 2000
First published in Great Britain in 2007
First paperback publication 2008

A CIP catalogue record for this book is
available from the British Library.

ISBN 978 1 84362 702 9 (hardback)
ISBN 978 1 84362 711 1 (paperback)

1 3 5 7 9 10 8 6 4 2 (hardback)
1 3 5 7 9 10 8 6 4 2 (paperback
Printed in Great Britain
Orchard Books is a division of Hachette Children's Books,
an Hachette Livre UK company.
www.orchardbooks.co.uk

DRAGLINS LOST!

VIVIAN FRENCH CHRIS FISHER

ORCHARD BOOKS

CHAPTER ONE

Dennis was flinging his possessions round his bedroom.

"Where IS it?" he muttered, and dived underneath his sleeping mat. When Dora appeared in the doorway, all she could see were his feet.

"What are you doing?" she asked. "We're going to be late for school if you don't hurry!"

Dennis struggled out and glared at her. "I can't come 'til I've found Slump's bootball. He lent it to me yesterday, and I PROMISED I'd bring it back today!"

"Danny and Daffodil are playing bootball by the front door," Dora told him. "Maybe they've got it."

"WHAT?" Dennis shot past her. "I'll KILL them! They never asked if they could borrow it!"

*

Dora sighed as she heard sounds of battle from outside Under Shed. She enjoyed school, but it was so difficult to get there on time. Every morning she hoped that she, Daffodil, Danny and Dennis would get there early so she could talk to her friend Violet before school began, but it never happened. She was lucky if they arrived before the bell went; usually they scraped in as Mrs Gage was taking the register.

Dora trailed back to the kitchen. Aunt Plum, who was trying to persuade Pip to take his cough mixture, saw her face. "At least they're all outside now," she said encouragingly. "Oh, don't forget to tell Mrs Gage that Pip's not at all well today."

Pip coughed loudly.

"Poor little Pip." Dora gave her small cousin a kiss. "Are the uncles around? I haven't said goodbye to them."

"They've gone Collecting," Aunt Plum said. "They went off into the Underground early this morning – Uncle Plant says they might bring back some peazles!"

Dora trotted out of the house trying not to worry. She liked to have all her family – Aunt Plum, Uncle Damson, Uncle Plant and Uncle Puddle, Pip and her brothers and sister – safely at home, where she could keep an eye on them. Outdoors was full of dangers, and although Under Shed was well hidden by an old and dilapidated garden shed covered in brambles and ivy, Dora always feared the worst. She had spent the first years of her life at the top of a safe warm tenement flat, and the move to the uncles' house had given her hundreds more things to worry about. Dennis and Daffodil, who thought Under Roof was the most boring place in the whole wide world, had been thrilled by the move, and Danny had been pleased as well. It was only Dora who spent her time agonising over all the dreadful things that could happen.

"The uncles will be safe if they all keep together," she told herself. "At least – I hope they will."

Dora found Dennis, Danny and Daffodil

still in a squirming heap. Asking them to stop had no effect at all, so in desperation she decided to try a trick that sometimes worked when Pip wouldn't do what he was told. Heading for the Underground, she called back over her shoulder, "I've got a secret!"

At once the fight broke up, and her sister and brothers raced after her, Dennis clutching Slump's precious football.

"What? What is it?" Dennis panted.

"The uncles have gone to collect peazles," Dora said.

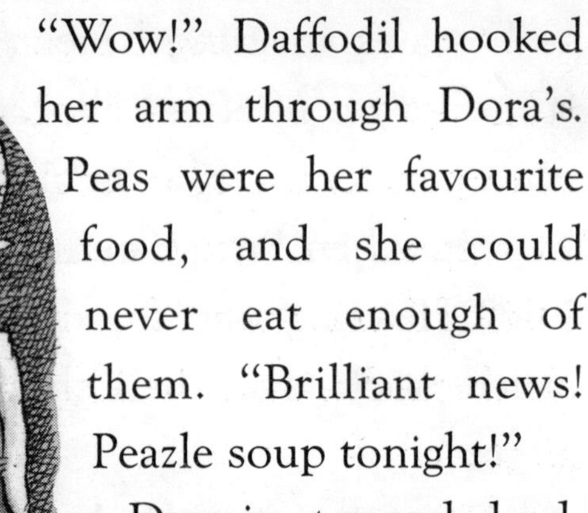

"Wow!" Daffodil hooked her arm through Dora's. Peas were her favourite food, and she could never eat enough of them. "Brilliant news! Peazle soup tonight!"

Dennis stopped dead, and began straightening his spectacles. "That's not much of a secret," he complained. "I thought it would be something interesting."

Danny, who knew how Dora's mind worked, grinned at him. "Dor wants to get to school," he explained.

Dennis frowned. "I'm not Pip," he said crossly.

Dora felt it would be unwise to say that sometimes he was far more trouble than Pip. "If we hurry, we might get there before the bell goes," she encouraged, but Dennis went on fiddling with his glasses and didn't move.

Danny, who liked school almost as much

as Dora did, slapped Dennis on the back. "Thought you were going to challenge Slump to a kicking match?"

"Dennis can't kick nearly as far as I can," Daffodil interrupted, and seizing the ball she kicked it into the Underground as hard as she could.

"OI!" Dennis yelled, and charged after it, Daffodil close behind him.

"Phew!" Danny said, and he and Dora hurried after them.

SCHOOL CLOSED
TODAY. ONE DAY
HOLIDAY. SEE YOU
ALL TOMORROW!
Mrs. Gage
P.S. If you're reading this
note you can't have been
paying attention during
last Tuesday's assembly!

CHAPTER TWO

They arrived outside the school gate puffing hard. Violet was sitting on the ground in floods of tears, but there was no sign of anyone else, and the school front door was firmly shut.

"Hey! What's going on?" Daffodil asked. "Where is everybody?"

"I don't KNOW!" Violet wailed. "I got here late because I couldn't find my homework and I thought Mrs Gage would be really cross and there was nobody here and I didn't know what to do!"

"H'mph," Daffodil said, and stormed past her to the door. "Look! There's a note! Didn't you read it, Violet?"

"I didn't see it." Violet sniffed hard as Dora put her arm round her shoulders and gave her a hankie. "I thought everyone had been eaten by a horrible great big chat."

Daffodil rolled her eyes, and read the note out loud.

SCHOOL CLOSED TODAY.
ONE DAY HOLIDAY. SEE YOU ALL TOMORROW!
Mrs Gage
P.S. If you're reading this note you can't have been paying attention during last Tuesday's assembly!

The little draglins looked at each other.

"We were late last Tuesday," Danny said at last. "Don't you remember? Daffy's beetle got out, and we had to catch him, and we arrived after assembly was over."

"But I was there." Violet frowned. Suddenly her face cleared, and she gave a nervous giggle. "Oh yes...Mrs Gage did say something about a holiday, but I was looking out of the window for you, Dora, and I didn't hear what day it was, and then I forgot."

Dennis wasn't listening to Violet. He was jumping up and down in excitement. "This is so GREAT!" he chortled. "Just think! It means we've got a whole day to do exactly what we like! We can go exploring!"

Dora looked horrified. "But we have to go home!"

"Why?" Daffodil asked. "No one'll be expecting us until home time. Come on, Dor – we can have FUN!"

"You can come to my house, if you like," Violet suggested hopefully. "Then I won't have to go home on my own." She shuddered. "It's very scary, because there's always lots of human beanies in the peazle field."

Dennis and Daffodil immediately looked as if they'd won a prize.

"WE'RE not scared of ANYTHING!" Dennis folded his arms, and beamed at Violet.

"That's right!" Daffodil agreed. "We'll take you home, and then we'll go and Collect some peazles." She ignored Dora's anxious squeaks, and went on trying to impress the wide-eyed Violet. "We like to do our own Collecting, you see."

"WOW!" Violet was breathless with admiration. "My mum says I can't go Collecting until I'm grown up." Her eyes filled with tears again. "My dad had an accident when he was Collecting, and he never came home, so that makes her worried."

Dora squeezed her hand. "Poor you," she said kindly.

"We don't have a mum OR a dad." Dennis was tactlessly cheerful. "Just Aunt Plum and a load of uncles. Which way do you go?"

Violet pointed behind the school. "That way – down the Underground."

"Brilliant! We've never been down that bit." Dennis tucked the bootball under his arm. "Let's move!"

Danny saw Dora's pale face. "It'll be OK, Dor," he said kindly. "And you'd like to see Violet safely home, wouldn't you?"

Dora reluctantly nodded, and the party set off, Violet leading the way.

CHAPTER THREE

Although the four little draglins from Under Shed had explored a good deal of the Underground, Dennis was right when he said they'd never been along the branch that led away from the school towards the strips of land where vegetables and flowers grew. The humans who worked there called them the Greyhouse allotments, but the draglins called them the peazle fields, and there were a number of draglin houses hidden close by. It was easy to Collect food, and the small sheds scattered over the area had the most exciting contents. There were crusts from sandwiches, crumbs of cake, apple cores and delicious seeds – not to mention the pieces of wood, nails, string and other prizes.

Dennis and Daffodil spent the journey boasting about how much they would

Collect, while Dora chatted to Violet. Danny found himself staring at the walls of the long dim tunnel. They were smoother and more finished than the tunnels he was used to, and the floor under his feet was almost polished.

"Must have been loads and LOADS of draglins along here," he thought. "Wonder why they don't come our way?"

Before he could wonder any more Violet stopped, and said in a hushed whisper, "Look! There's the Outdoors! And that's my house over there – do you think it's safe to cross?"

The draglins gathered at the Underground entrance, and looked with interest at what was outside. Instead of grass, as there was outside Under Shed, there was a sea of mud.

Stepping stones led the way across to a fence, but weeds and brambles grew so thickly in between the posts that it took the Under Shed draglins a moment or two to spot the row of neat front doors hidden amongst the twisted stalks.

"Hey!" Daffodil said loudly. "You've got NEIGHBOURS! That's cool!"

"Sssssh!" Violet put her finger to her lips. "There are nearly always Beanies on the other side – that's where the peazle fields are!"

And as if she had called it up, the figure of a tall man strode past on the other side of the fence, a spade over his shoulder. Violet shrieked and rushed into the Underground, but the others shrank silently into the shadows.

Daffodil was the first one out. "Hey!" she called. "It's all clear now! Let's cross!"

"Mind you don't step in the mud," Violet warned her. "Mum says we must NEVER leave footprints!"

Daffodil snorted, and jumped neatly from

stepping stone to stepping stone.

"I'm not silly," she remarked coldly as she reached the shelter of the fence.

Violet blushed, and waited for Danny, Dennis and Dora before she hopped across herself.

"Thank you VERY much," she said as she paused outside her front door. "Are you sure you don't want to come and play?"

"Dora can if she wants," Daffodil said grandly. "The rest of us are going to explore, and Collect things."

Violet looked at Dora, who slowly shook her head. "I'd better stay with them," she said. "But I'd love to come another time."

"OK," Violet told her, and turned her door handle...

...but the door wouldn't open.

Violet looked worried. She tried again, and again, but the door was shut fast.

"Mum must have gone out," she said, her voice wobbling badly. "I can't get in! What shall I do?"

"You'll have to come with us," Daffodil told her, with a marked lack of enthusiasm.

Dora took Violet's hand. "I'll look after you," she said.

"You won't be doing dangerous things, will you?" Violet was trembling.

"No," Dora promised.

"Yes," Dennis said at exactly the same moment, but Danny coughed, and Violet didn't hear.

Dennis was itching to get on with his adventure. He squared his shoulders, and picked up a long stick. "Are you lot ready? Where shall we start?"

"Please, Dennis – couldn't we take Violet back to Under Shed?" Dora asked with a shiver. "That Beanie was HUGE."

"But he was busy doing Beanie stuff," Daffodil told her. "He won't be bothered with us."

Dora wasn't convinced. "What if he's got a dawg?"

Violet squealed, and Dennis shrugged in a So What kind of way. Danny, however, looked thoughtful. "It's a good point," he said, "we ought to be extra careful. Let's listen – Aunt Plum says beanies are always whistling or shouting at dawgs."

The five little draglins froze into silence.

They could hear nothing unusual. No whistling, or shouting, or barking.

"Seems all right to me," Danny said. He squinted up at the sun. "We can't be too long, anyway. We can't risk being late back."

Daffodil followed his gaze. "We've got AGES yet," she said. "The sun's not even overhead!"

Dora sighed, and she and the quivering Violet followed Dennis, Danny and Daffodil as they pushed their way through the undergrowth, and so to the edge of the allotments. As the first weeds began to close behind her, Dora glanced back. "I MUST remember where the Underground entrance is," she told herself. "It would be really TERRIBLE if we couldn't find it again!" Then she hurried to catch up with Danny, pulling Violet with her.

CHAPTER FOUR

Dennis was striding out in front, determined to show Violet what a big and brave draglin he was. Daffodil, marching along behind him, was annoyed. She knew he was showing off, but she couldn't see why he would want to impress such a weedy little draglin. She put on a burst of speed and overtook him.

Dennis began to run.

Daffodil ran faster...

"Oi!" From behind Danny called as loudly as he dared. "You two! Slow down!"

But Dennis and Daffodil didn't hear him. They were running as fast as they could go over the rough earth, dodging in between tall spikes of green leaves and jumping the stones.

Dennis was hampered by carrying the football, and gradually Daffodil drew further and further ahead. As she sprinted in between the onions and carrots a triumphant smile spread over her face.

"That'll show him!" she said, and she swung herself behind a particularly tufty carrot and crouched down. "AND I'll give him a fright when he zooms past!"

But Dennis had given up. He had a stitch in his side, and his eyes, unused to bright sunlight, were hurting. If Violet had been watching he would have kept going until his last gasp, but she was nowhere near.

"Daffy? DAFFY!" he called. "I'm not racing any more!"

There was no answer. Daffodil, silently hugging herself with glee, was determined not to give her hiding place away.

"DAFFODIL! Where are you?" Dennis was almost shouting as he hurried first one way and then the other. When there was still no answer, he shook his head. "Bet she's playing some stupid game. Well, I'M going to go back to Danny and the others." He began to walk...and then stopped. The spiked leaves of onions and fluffy green carrot tops surrounded him, and he realised he had no idea which way he had come.

"DRAT Daffodil!" Dennis said crossly. "This is all her fault! I'll have to find somewhere to climb so I can see where I am."

He tried to swing his way up a clump of onion leaves, but they weren't strong enough

to hold his weight. Muttering to himself, he chose the largest onion he could find, and balanced on top of its smooth round curve. It wasn't very high, but he was sure he could see a glimpse of taller greenery not too far away. "Hurrah!" he thought. "Dennis wins again!" And forgetting all about his stick and the football, he set off as fast as he could run.

Daffodil went on waiting. It wasn't long before she got bored, and stood up. Seeing no sign of Dennis, she rubbed her nose thoughtfully. "Maybe he's hiding from me?" she said to herself. "Or has he just given up?" Her tummy rumbled, and she realised she was hungry. "Time to find some peazles," she decided. "Now, do I find them for myself, or do I go with the others?"

Being Daffodil, she found no problem in making the decision. "I'll find my own, but I'll pick enough for the others as well. There's no way that weedy little Violet is ever going to let them have an adventure. Now, which way shall I go?" She rubbed her nose again. "The sun was on my face when we came out of the Underground, so if it's on my back I'll find the fence. I'll go along the edge a bit until I find the peazles..." And Daffodil turned round, and trotted confidently in between the plants.

She hadn't gone far when something caught her eye. "That's Slump's bootball! And Dennis's stick! So he must have been here – but why's he left them?" Puzzled, she picked up the ball. "S'pose I'd better bring this with me. Can't be bothered with his silly stick, though." And she trotted on.

CHAPTER FIVE

A few minutes later she found herself back at the fence, but before she had a chance to move on and find her way to the peazles a small figure dashed from behind a dandelion leaf and hugged her so tightly she could hardly breathe.

"GERROFFF!" Daffodil pushed Dora away. "What are you doing here?"

"Oh, Daffy!" Dora tried to hug her sister again. "We didn't know where you'd got to! We tried and tried to keep up with you, but you went so fast – and then Violet began to cry because she was so scared, and we came back to the fence."

"That's right!" Violet crept out, her eyes still red. "We thought you were DEAD!"

Danny appeared beside Dora, looking angry. "Honestly, Daffodil!" he said. "How STUPID can you be, running off like that?"

He paused, and looked expectantly over her shoulder. "Where's Dennis?"

Daffodil shrugged. She was beginning to realise she shouldn't have ignored Dennis when he called out to her, and guilt made her bad tempered. "How should I know?" She put the football down on the ground. "He left this by an onion."

Dora and Danny stared at Daffodil, their mouths open in shock. Violet burst into tears again.

"You mean," Danny said slowly, "that you came back here WITHOUT Dennis? But you were racing each other! What happened?"

Daffodil was feeling worse and worse, but she was not going to admit she had done anything wrong. "He must have run the wrong way," she said. "Stupid him."

"But didn't you LOOK for him?" Danny couldn't believe his ears. "Didn't you even TRY and find him?"

Daffodil lost her temper. "I don't know WHERE he is," she shouted. "And I'M going to find some peazles, so THERE!" And she stamped away, trying her hardest to stop the angry and frustrated tears from trickling down her face.

Violet grabbed Dora's arm, and pointed in the opposite direction.

"But the peazles are over there!" she sobbed. "Daffodil's going the wrong way!"

"Quick!" Dora said. "We've got to follow her. Come on, Danny – you know what she's like!"

Danny did know. Luckily Daffodil was too upset to go very fast, and they were able to keep her easily in sight until she flung herself down amongst some daisies to thump the ground with her fists, and cry.

Dora took a deep breath. Of all the adventures she had ever been on, this was turning out to be one of the worst. Someone had to do something.

"Don't nag Daffodil any more," she told Danny. "Let's try and make a plan – we've GOT to find Dennis!"

"But he's LOST!" Violet wailed. "He's lost in the middle of that great big peazle field, and we'll never see him again!"

The peaceful Dora turned on Violet. "PLEASE try and stop whining!" she snapped. "You're making things worse! Daffy's crying because she's feeling so awful about losing Dennis, and we've got to do something about it!"

Violet was so surprised she did as she was told. Dora's hankie was soaking wet, so she wiped her eyes and her nose on her sleeve. "Sorry," she said, and then, "shall I carry the bootball for you?"

"OK," Dora said, and handed it over.

Danny had gone to squat down beside Daffodil. "Come on, Daffy," he said. "You're the brainy one. How are we going to find Dennis?"

"Go away!" Daffodil buried her face in the daisies.

Danny sighed, and sat back on his heels.

Daffodil stayed where she was, but her brain was racing. She had been trying to convince herself that Dennis was busy with some plan of his own, but she was now almost sure he was lost. Pictures kept popping into her mind that she didn't want to see; pictures of Dennis being eaten by a dawg, or carried away by a chat who had mistaken him for a mowser.

Then, suddenly, she had an idea. A brilliant idea. An idea that made her want to pat herself on the back, and cheer.

"Danny," she said as she sat up. "Where's the bootball?"

Danny looked at Daffodil in astonishment. "Violet's looking after it," he said. "Why?"

Daffodil scrambled to her feet, her eyes shining. "We can use it to help Dennis find us!" she said.

"HOW?" Danny asked.

"If we kick it up into the air," Daffodil said, "he'll see it – and he'll know which way to come and find us!"

Danny, who had been hoping Daffodil's idea would be sensible, sank down on the grass, his head in his hands. "And every Human Beanie for miles around will see it too," he said.

"Actually – they might not." To Danny's amazement, Dora was beaming at Daffodil. "I think it's worth a try!"

CHAPTER SIX

Dennis was fed up. He felt as if he'd been running for ages, and he could still see nothing but carrots and onions. As he slowed to walking pace, he realised he'd left his stick and Slump's bootball behind.

"I'll see it when I find something to climb," he thought. "I'll keep going for – OH! Oh NO!"

His stomach lurched uncomfortably. In front of him was a particularly large onion, and leaning against it was his stick. There was no sign of the bootball. Dennis gulped, and sat down on the onion.

"I must have been going in a circle," he thought. "And Daffy must have come to look for me, and found the bootball...oh dear." He swallowed hard. "But I'm not lost. I'm NOT. It's just...I just haven't quite found the right way to go."

"ARRRRRK!"

Dennis jumped. The most enormous bird he had ever seen was staring at him hungrily, first with one black beady eye, and then the other. Dennis grabbed his stick, and backed slowly and steadily round behind the onion.

The crow followed him.

"Keep cool," Dennis told himself. "Brids don't eat draglins. Uncle Damson said so..."

He took a firmer grip on his stick, and stood still, although his heart was beating so hard he was certain he must be shaking.

The crow stopped too.

There was a minute movement in the earth in front of Dennis. With a sudden twist of its gleaming head and one swift slice of its big black beak, the crow snatched up a wriggling worm. Still keeping one sharp eye on Dennis, it threw its head back and swallowed.

The worm vanished.

"Ugh," Dennis said.

"ARRRK" said the crow, and hopped closer. Dennis jumped on the onion, and waved his stick wildly.

"GET AWAY!" he yelled, not caring who could hear him. Anything – even a Human Beanie – was better than being eaten like a worm. "SHOVE OFF! GO AWAY! LEAVE ME ALONE!"

At once the crow moved backwards, shaking its feathers.

"YAH! SHOOOO!" Dennis shrieked. "THAT'S IT! MOVE OFF!" And thinking he was winning, he leapt down and charged forwards, swinging his stick round and round his head.

The bird blinked, there was a sharp CRACK! and Dennis's stick was gone. With a howl of terror he dashed behind the onion and crouched down, his heart hammering so hard he could hardly breathe.

"That's it," he thought. "I'm going to be eaten..."

At the edge of the allotments Dora and Dennis shook and went pale as Dennis's howl faintly reached them. Daffodil, hot and sweaty from her many attempts to kick the bootball high in the air, felt a cold chill sweep over her.

"Oh no..." she whispered.

Violet looked at her friends, and saw they were thinking the worst. Her eyes filled with tears, but she dashed them away. "I must DO something," she thought. "They're so BRAVE!" and she ran at the bootball. As she reached it, she shut her eyes tightly, and kicked as hard as she could…

…and the ball soared up in the air, and away and away.

CHAPTER SEVEN

Dennis crept out from behind the onion, rubbed his eyes, and then rubbed them again. Two coal black feathers fluttered on the ground in front of him, but the crow had gone – and beside the feathers was Slump's ball.

He shook his head, and tried to make sense of what had happened. He had been so certain that his last second had come that he had scrunched himself down, hardly breathing, just waiting for the attack. But then had come a THUMP! and a furious and indignant ARRRRRK! This had been followed by the clatter of wings...and silence.

"Daffy?" he said wonderingly. "DAFFY?"

Nothing.

Dennis picked up the feathers and the football, and stared round. "If I could work out where it came from," he thought, "I'd know which way to go..."

He felt the back of his neck. "Phew! It's hot. Next thing I'll be dying of sunburn. At least it'll be nice and cool once I get back to the Underground – IF I can get back... WHAT WAS THAT?"

His ears straining, he listened again. It had sounded like a shriek, or a yell, but it wasn't repeated. Dennis hesitated, then set off in the direction the sound had come from. "That horrible onion is behind me, and so is the sun," he worked out as he walked. And then, "Of course! If I keep following my shadow I won't go round in a circle again! Why didn't I think of that before?"

Five minutes later he saw the fence, and began to run... and Violet, balanced on Daffodil's shoulders, began to scream with excitement. "I can see him! He's COMING!" Daffodil, who was perilously balanced on Danny and Dora's linked arms, forgot all about Violet and jumped.

Violet, Danny and Dora collapsed in a heap and, as Dennis came hurrying up arm in arm with a glowing Daffodil, they were rubbing bumps and bruises, but grinning madly.

"Here I am!" Dennis said. He waved the feathers. "Had a bit of a ruckus with a brid, but it was fine. I scared him off." A sudden flashback made him add, "Of course, Daffy's brilliant bootball technique helped. Whacked him on the head!" He slapped Daffodil's back. "I'll tell Slump you've got to be on the bootball team!"

Daffodil went pink, then red, and then purple. "It wasn't me," she said at last. "It was Violet."

Dennis began to laugh. "Oh, yeah," he said. "And Human Beanies can fly!"

"It's true," Danny told him, and Dora nodded.

"WOW!" Dennis looked at Violet admiringly, and she blushed. "Hey – do you fancy playing in the match next week?"

Violet shook her head. "No thank you,"

she said shyly. "Let Daffodil play. She's MUCH better than me – I didn't even mean to kick it that way. I'll come and watch, though."

"I'll come with you," Dora said. She gave an anxious glance up at the sun. "Erm – shouldn't we be thinking of going back home now?"

"But we haven't got any peazles yet!" Daffodil was aghast. "That's why we came here in the first place!"

Dennis was about to agree with her, but changed his mind at the last minute. He suddenly realised he was tired. VERY tired. And the thought of going back into the field made him feel even worse. "We could come

here after school," he said. He twirled the bootball on his finger in a casual, devil-may-care manner. "Why don't we walk back with Violet tomorrow, and then go peazling?"

Dora and Danny stared at him in astonishment, Daffodil in horror.

Violet wriggled, and blushed again. "You could all have tea with me," she said. "Mum won't mind. She'll make peazle pie if you like."

Daffodil brightened. "REALLY?" she asked. "D'you promise?"

Violet nodded.

"OK, then." Daffodil hesitated, and then smiled. "You know – it WAS a good kick, Violet."

CHAPTER EIGHT

Having seen Violet safely home, the four Under Shed draglins plodded back along the Underground. They were unusually quiet. Dora was worrying that they were going to be late, and Danny was thinking about food. Dennis had his own private thoughts, and Daffodil was becoming conscious of an uncomfortable feeling.

"My ears feel hot," she said.

"That's odd." Dennis frowned. "So do mine! Do you think it's because we're hungry?"

"I'm starving," Danny said, "but my ears are OK. It's my stomach that isn't. I do hope Aunt Plum's got something nice for our tea."

Dora paused, and looked at Dennis and Daffodil's ears. Even in the dim light of the tunnel there was a curious glow about them.

"You do look a bit weird," she said. "We'll ask Aunt Plum."

"Do you think she'll let us off school tomorrow?" Daffodil said hopefully. "If she did, we could go straight to the fields!"

"But then we wouldn't see Vi—" Dennis began, and then stopped.

Dora, Danny and Daffodil were all three looking at him with exactly the same expression on their faces.

"Did I tell you the brid chased me round

and round the onion?" he said quickly. "I was nearly eaten!"

It wasn't any good. Danny gave a long whistle, Dora smiled, and Daffodil sniggered.

"You like Violet!" she said, and blew kisses into the air.

"I do NOT!" Dennis said furiously. "I just said – oh, BOTHER it!" And he stormed off ahead so his sisters and brother had to run to keep up with him.

*

As the four draglins popped out of the Underground and trotted across the grass to Under Shed, they saw Aunt Plum standing in the doorway, Pip in her arms.

"You're very late," she told them. "I was beginning to get anxious."

"Sorry," Daffodil said breezily. "We had to take Violet home. Is tea ready?"

Aunt Plum didn't answer. She was gazing at Daffodil's ears. "You've got SUNBURNT!" she said. "WHEREVER have you been? You too, Dennis. Whatever have you been doing?"

Dennis and Daffodil both began to speak at the same time, and changed it into a fit of coughing. Danny stepped forward.

"School didn't finish at the usual time," he said truthfully. "So we went back to Violet's house, and it was by the peazle fields... Hey, Aunt Plum – Violet's FANTASTIC at bootball!"

Dora nodded enthusiastically. "She can kick for MILES!"

"H'm." Aunt Plum didn't look convinced, but she didn't ask any more questions. "Go and wash your hands," she said. "The uncles have brought back something REALLY special!"

"PEAZLES!" shouted Daffodil. "Hurrah!"

"No dear," Aunt Plum said. "It's even better. They've rolled three huge onions all the way down the Underground, so we've got onion soup tonight, and onion pie tomorrow, and it'll be onion mash the day after. Dennis, are you all right? You're looking very pale..."

HAVE YOU READ ALL THE DRAGLINS BOOKS?

Daffodil, Dora, Dennis and Danny can't believe they are moving to the great Outdoors! How will they get down from Under Roof? And will they get to see the scary chats and dawgs they've heard so much about?

Daffodil, Dora, Dennis and Danny have moved Outdoors, but their things are trapped Under Roof! Dennis has a PLAN to rescue them… But will the gigantic Human Beanies get in the way?

Wowling has been heard near the draglins' home in Under Shed! Daffodil, Dora, Dennis and Danny come face to face with a scary chat for the first time ever – are four little draglins a match for terrible teeth and sharp claws?

What will draglin school in the great Outdoors be like? Daffodil, Dora, Dennis and Danny don't know what to expect, but their classmate Peg does. She wants to be boss!

Human Beanies are dangerous, especially when they're blowing smoke. Now there's a fire in Under Shed, and the flames are spreading! Can Daffodil, Dora, Dennis and Danny save their home?

Daffodil, Dora, Dennis and Danny are off to visit Great Grandmother Attica, but it's a scary journey. Can they save themselves, let alone a little ducklet lost on the edge of the Great Wetness?

Summer holidays should be fun, but it hasn't rained in weeks. There are cracks in the Underground, and Daffodil, Dora, Dennis and Danny's world is in terrible danger – what can they do?

by Vivian French
illustrated by Chris Fisher

Draglins Escape	978 1 84362 705 0
Draglins to the Rescue	978 1 84362 706 7
Draglins and the Flood	978 1 84362 707 4
Draglins in Danger	978 1 84362 708 1
Draglins and the Bully	978 1 84362 709 8
Draglins and the Fire	978 1 84362 710 4
Draglins Lost	978 1 84362 711 1
Draglins Find a Hero	978 1 84362 712 8

All priced at £3.99.

Draglins books are available from all good bookshops,
or can be ordered direct from the publisher:
Orchard Books, PO BOX 29, Douglas IM99 1BQ.
Credit card orders please telephone 01624 836000
or fax 01624 837033 or visit our website:
www.orchardbooks.co.uk
or e-mail: bookshop@enterprise.net for details.

To order please quote title, author and ISBN
and your full name and address.
Cheques and postal orders should be made
payable to 'Bookpost plc.'

Postage and packing is FREE within the UK
(overseas customers should add £2.00 per book).

Prices and availability are subject to change.